FIRESTORM CAMPFIRE TALES

MM MYERS

Contents

Firestorm Campfire Stories

Copyright © 2025 Firestorm Publishing LLC

ISBN: 979-8-9922064-2-5

Dedication

To all those who gather 'round the campfire, sharing stories that send shivers down our spines and ignite our imaginations.

To Doc Price, troop 15, Norfolk, VA, the first BSA troop leader, for my sons, whose spirit of adventure inspired generations.

And to Cece Johnson, thank you for always being my sounding board, sharing your thoughts, and reminding me of the magic in every tale.

Love you!

About the Author

Mary Myers is a natural-born storyteller who has captivated her children and grandchildren for years with her imaginative tales. Though putting pen to paper has been challenging, Mary has persevered in her dream of sharing her stories with the world.

With the help of technology and the encouragement of her supportive family, Mary has embarked on a new chapter as a published author. Her heartfelt stories, infused with gratitude and an abiding faith, offer readers a glimpse into the rich inner life of this passionate and enthusiastic storyteller.

Mary's journey from reluctant writer to published author is a testament to the power of determination and the gift of a vibrant, creative mind.

The Haunted Mobility Cart; A Spine-Chilling Tale

I don't usually write Halloween stories, but the other day, I didn't have my own cart and had to use Walmart's; it was a horrible ride; it would start then stop out of nowhere... and so this story came to my mind...

Again, it's just a story, and the Devine Walmart, at least to the best of my knowledge, does not have mobility carts that are possessed. They may feel like it from time to time, but that's another story for yet another time.....

In the town of Devine, nestled among the shadowy trees, a Walmart with a dark secret stood erect and undaunting. It was whispered among the locals that the shopping mobility carts that roamed the store had become vessels for restless spirits, trapped between the realms of the living and the dead.

One fateful day, Grandma Mary ventured into Walmart to collect her prescription. Little did she know that her trip would plunge her into a spine-chilling nightmare.

An ominous chill filled the air as Mary settled into one of the shopping mobility carts. The moment she activated the cart, it sprang to life with an evil energy. It began to move erratically, jerking forward and halting abruptly as if possessed by an unseen force.

Terrified shoppers scrambled to get out of the cart's path, but its movements were unpredictable, causing chaos and panic. People stumbled and fell, unaware of the invisible hands that seemed to push and pull them into harm's way.

Mary's heart pounded in her chest as she desperately tried to regain control.

"Watch out! Beware of the runaway cart!" she cried out, her voice drowned by the cacophony of screams and commotion. But her warnings went unanswered as the cart continued its relentless rampage.

With each passing moment, the cart's malevolence intensified. It surged forward, propelling Mary through the aisles at a breakneck speed. She clung to the cart's handle, her knuckles turning white, as she pleaded for her life.

But her pleas fell on deaf ears. The cart seemed possessed by a vengeful spirit, determined to wreak havoc on anyone in its path. It careened through the store, knocking over displays and leaving destruction in its wake. The once familiar aisles had transformed into a nightmarish labyrinth.

Just when Mary thought she could bear the terror no longer, the cart halted abruptly. The Walmart manager, alerted by the chaos, rushed to her rescue. But as Mary began to breathe a sigh of relief, the cart reawakened with a sinister intent.

Without warning, it lunged forward once again, propelling Mary backward with a force that defied explanation. Her hands flailed in the air, nowhere near the controls, as she fought to regain her balance. The cart, relentless in its pursuit, seemed determined to claim her life.

The Walmart employees, their faces etched with fear, banded together in a desperate attempt to stop the cart's reign of terror. They dodged its path, their hearts pounding with adrenaline, as they strategized on how to save Mary from the clutches of this unholy machine.

Finally, with a collective surge of courage, they managed to bring the possessed cart to a stop. Silence descended upon Walmart, broken only by the sound of heavy breathing and the distant wails of distant spirits.

Mary, shaken and bruised, was helped to her feet by the Walmart manager. Their eyes met, and in that moment, both knew they had witnessed something far more sinister than a mere malfunctioning cart. The veil between the living and the dead had been lifted, revealing a haunting truth.

From that day forward, the legend of the possessed shopping mobility cart at Walmart in Devine spread like wildfire. It became a chilling tale of caution, a reminder to all who ventured into the store that unseen forces lurked in the most unexpected places.

As Halloween approached each year, the townspeople would gather, huddled around flickering candlelight, to recount the harrowing tale of Mary's encounter with the vicious cart. The story served as a chilling reminder that in the darkest corners of our world, the line between the living and the dead could blur, unleashing unspeakable horrors upon the unsuspecting.

And so, Walmart in Devine became a place of whispered tales and lingering fear, forever haunted by the memory of that fateful day when a simple shopping trip turned into a nightmare of supernatural proportions.

Beware, for no one knows when and if it will return! Hang on tightly, for the ride may be your last!

Echoes Of the Past

The night was cold, and still; the only sounds were the eerie creaking of old oak trees and the occasional hoot of an owl. Down a winding dirt road just outside the small town of Moore, Texas, a shadowy figure moved through the darkness, its form indistinct, yet unmistakably that of a rider upon a horse.

As the figure drew closer, a chill ran down the spines of any unfortunate souls who were out on this moonless night. For this was no ordinary rider - it was the Headless Horseman of Moore, a terrifying specter that had haunted these roads for generations, striking fear into the hearts of all who encountered it.

The legend of the Headless Horseman began over a century ago, during the tumultuous Texas Revolution. Moore, a sleepy farming community, had found itself caught in the crossfire as Texian and Mexican forces clashed over control of the Alamo. Tensions ran high, and violence often erupted without warning.

One fateful night, a young Texian soldier named Juan Hernandez was out on patrol, guarding the perimeter of the town. As he rode his horse down the old dirt road, Juan was ambushed by a group of Mexican loyalists. A fierce struggle ensued, and in the chaos, Juan was struck in the neck by a stray musket ball, his head severed from his body.

Juan's lifeless form tumbled from the saddle, his horse galloping off into the night, leaving the headless corpse behind. The townspeople who discovered the grisly scene were horrified, and rumors quickly spread that Juan's spirit, unable to find peace, had risen from the grave to haunt the very road where he had met his end.

And so, the legend of the Headless Horseman of Moore was born, and over the years, countless sightings of the ghostly rider have been reported by those brave or foolish enough to venture down that dark, winding road after sunset.

Some say the Horseman is doomed to ride eternally, his spectral form searching for his lost head. Others claim he is a harbinger of doom, his appearance a harbinger of death and misfortune.

And there are those who believe the Horseman embodies the violent and turbulent history that has shaped this small Texas town.

On this particular night, young Jenna, a local high school student, found herself driving down the old Moore Road, her car's headlights cutting through the inky blackness. Jenna had heard the stories, of course, but like so many before her, she couldn't resist the allure of the Headless Horseman legend...

As Jenna's car crept down the dark, winding road, a thick fog began to roll in, obscuring her vision. Suddenly, a shadowy figure emerged from the mist - the unmistakable silhouette of a rider on horseback. Jenna's heart raced as she realized she was face-to-face with the legendary Headless Horseman.

The ghostly figure drew closer, its horse's hooves thundering against the dirt. Jenna gripped the steering wheel, torn between the urge to floor the gas and flee, and her overwhelming curiosity to get a better look at the terrifying specter.

Just as the Horseman reached her car, Jenna caught a glimpse of its fearsome, faceless form. A chill ran down her spine, and she let out a terrified gasp. The Horseman paused momentarily, as if sensing her presence, then continued on its ghostly ride, disappearing back into the swirling fog.

Shaken but unharmed, Jenna sat in her car, trying to make sense of what she had just witnessed. She knew the stories, of course - how the Headless Horseman was said to be the restless spirit of a Texian soldier killed during the Battle of the Alamo. But she had never expected to come face-to-face with the legend herself.

Determined to uncover the truth behind the Horseman's origins, Jenna decided to do some digging. She started by visiting the local historical society, poring over old newspapers and documents from the Texas Revolution era.

It was there that Jenna stumbled upon a forgotten account of the fateful night when the young Texian soldier, Juan Hernandez, had been killed on the very road she had just traversed. The details were chilling - how Juan had been ambushed by Mexican loyalists, his head severed by a stray musket ball.

Jenna felt a chill as she read the description of Juan's lifeless body, abandoned on the dark road as his horse fled into the night. *Could this be the true origin of the Headless Horseman legend? Was Juan's restless spirit doomed to ride these roads for eternity, searching for his lost head?*

Determined to uncover the truth, Jenna began to investigate further, delving into the history of the Alamo and the tumultuous events that had shaped her town. She visited the site of the famous battle, walking the hallowed ground where so many had lost their lives in the fight for Texas independence.

As Jenna delved deeper into the past, she began to unravel the tangled web of events that had led to the creation of the Headless Horseman legend. She discovered that the violence and upheaval of the Texas Revolution had left deep scars on the community, and that the Horseman's haunting served as a grim reminder of the sacrifices made in the name of freedom.

But Jenna also uncovered something else - a glimmer of hope amidst the darkness.

For in the stories and legends of the Headless Horseman, she found a testament to the resilience and enduring spirit of the people of Moore.

Despite the horrors of the past, they persevered, and the legend of the Horseman had become a part of their collective identity, a symbol of the unbreakable strength that had carried them through even the darkest times.

As Jenna stood on the grounds of the Alamo, the weight of history heavy on her shoulders, she felt a newfound appreciation for the story of the Headless Horseman. It was not just a tale of terror, but a reflection of the human experience - of loss, suffering, and the indomitable power of the human spirit to overcome even the most daunting challenges.

And in that moment, Jenna knew that the legend of the Headless Horseman would continue to live on, a haunting reminder of the past and a testament to the enduring strength of the people of Moore, Texas.

The Halloween Biking Adventure

Once upon a time, a group of adventurous friends decided to embark on a thrilling biking adventure on a dark and eerie Halloween night. They had heard spooky tales about a haunted cemetery on the outskirts of town and fueled by their love for adrenaline rushes; they decided to explore it.

Decked out in their ghostly costumes and armed with flashlights, the group pedaled their bikes through the misty streets until they reached the entrance of the cemetery. The moon cast an eerie glow, adding an extra layer of spookiness to the atmosphere.

As they cautiously entered the graveyard, the friends couldn't help but feel a sense of trepidation. The gravestones loomed in the darkness like silent sentinels, and the wind whispered unsettling secrets through the trees. But their excitement pushed them forward.

They rode their bikes slowly along the winding paths, their tires crunching on fallen leaves and twigs. Every now and then, they let out nervous laughs, trying to shake off the growing unease.

In the midst of their adventure, one friend, let's call him Mike, spotted a massive and ornate gravestone. It stood tall and imposing, almost beckoning him to come closer. Driven by a mix of curiosity and bravado, Mike decided to ride his bike up to it.

Pedaling with determination, Mike approached the gravestone, his friends watching with bated breath. But just as he was about to triumphantly reach his destination, a hidden hole, covered by leaves and grass, appeared before him. With a sudden jolt, Mike's front tire sank into the hole, causing him to lose balance. He released a startled yelp as he tumbled off his bike and disappeared into the dark abyss.

His friends rushed to his aid, their laughter turning into concerned cries. But as they peered into the hole, expecting to see their fallen friend, they found it empty. Mike had vanished without a trace.

A shiver ran down their spines as they realized they were standing near an open grave. The legend of the cemetery had come to life, swallowing their friend whole. Fear gripped their hearts, and they knew they had to find him.

With their flashlights held tightly, they descended into the grave, one by one, hoping to uncover the mystery that had befallen their friend. But the deeper they went, the stranger things became. Shadows danced ominously around them, and eerie whispers echoed through the dimly lit tunnels.

Suddenly, they stumbled upon a hidden chamber filled with ancient artifacts and symbols. It was a secret underground passage, revealing a forgotten part of the cemetery's history. The friends realized Mike's fall had unearthed a long-lost secret, unleashing a chain of paranormal events.

Determined to rescue their friend and put an end to the curse, they followed the trail of clues deeper into the crypt. Along the way, they encountered restless spirits and faced spine-chilling challenges, testing their courage and unity.

After what felt like an eternity, they reached the heart of the crypt. There, they found Mike, shaken but unharmed. The friends quickly devised a plan to break the curse and set the spirits free.

Together, they performed a ritual, reciting ancient incantations and undoing the misfortune that had befallen the cemetery. As the last words left their lips, a blinding light filled the crypt, and the spirits were released, finding peace at long last.

Exhausted but victorious, the friends emerged from the crypt, their bond stronger than ever. They had survived a bone-chilling adventure and had a tale to tell for generations to come. From that day forward, they cherished Halloween as a reminder of the unforgettable night they rode their bikes into the cemetery and found more than they bargained for.

Shadow Wraith

Deep within the crumbling walls of an abandoned Victorian mansion, a group of daring teenagers gathered on the eve of Halloween, seeking an adrenaline rush and a taste of true terror. Legends whispered of an evil spirit haunting the decaying halls, known only as the Shadow Wraith.

As the clock struck midnight, the teenagers, armed with flashlights and trembling with anticipation, ventured into the darkness. The air grew thick with an otherworldly chill, and the sound of their own racing hearts drowned out the rustling of the wind through broken windows.

Room by room, they explored the mansion's haunted corridors, their footsteps echoing ominously. Tattered curtains danced eerily in the moonlight, and cobwebs clung to the walls like ghostly tapestries.

As they delved deeper into the mansion's secrets, a sense of foreboding settled upon them. Whispers echoed from hidden corners, their words too faint to discern but laden with malice. Shadows flickered along the walls, their movements defying all logic.

Suddenly, the atmosphere shifted. A hush fell over the teenagers as they felt an unseen presence envelop them. Their flashlights flickered and died, plunging them into impenetrable darkness. Panic gripped their hearts, for they knew they were no longer alone.

From the inky blackness emerged the form of the Shadow Wraith—a specter cloaked in tattered rags, its eyes glowing with an unearthly light. Its chilling laughter echoed through the mansion, freezing the blood of the brave souls who dared to challenge it.

The Shadow Wraith's supernatural powers manifested, manipulating the very fabric of reality. Objects levitated and spun wildly, defying gravity. Furniture shifted and crashed, trapping the terrified teenagers in a maze of treacherous debris.

One by one, the Shadow Wraith toyed with its prey. It whispered dark secrets, revealing their deepest fears and darkest desires. It lured them into treacherous illusions, distorting their perception of reality until they were lost in a nightmarish labyrinth of their own minds.

But among the chaos and despair, a flicker of resilience ignited within one of the teenagers. With unwavering determination, Sarah, the group's most fearless member, summoned her courage. She recalled an ancient chant passed down through generations; a chant said to banish even the most malevolent spirits. With trembling voice, Sarah recited the incantation, her words cutting through the cacophony of the Shadow Wraith's laughter. A blinding light erupted, forcing the specter to recoil in agony. The darkness retreated, and the mansion fell silent once more.

As the light faded, the teenagers found themselves standing outside the mansion, their hearts pounding with a mixture of relief and lingering dread. The Shadow Wraith had been vanquished, but its memory would haunt them forever.

From that night on, the abandoned Victorian mansion stood as a testament to their harrowing encounter, a place forever shrouded in mystery and whispered as a cautionary tale. The teenagers went their separate ways, forever bound by an unspoken bond forged in the crucible of terror.

And so, the legend of the Shadow Wraith and the haunted mansion persisted, a story shared among older kids on Halloween night, reminding them to tread carefully in the realm of the supernatural, for some horrors are better left undisturbed.

Remember, it's all just a spine-chilling tale, but let it serve as a reminder to approach the unknown cautiously. *Happy Halloween!*

The Demons of the Forbidden Chambers

Deep within the depths of an ancient, dilapidated cathedral, a group of intrepid explorers found themselves drawn to a forbidden chamber said to house an unspeakable evil. The air was heavy with a sense of impending doom as they ventured deeper into the labyrinthine catacombs beneath the sacred grounds. As they approached the chamber, a palpable darkness enveloped them. The flickering candlelight cast eerie shadows upon the cold stone walls, and a frigid breeze whispered through the narrow passageways. They knew they were entering a realm far beyond mortal comprehension.

With trepidation in their hearts, the explorers pushed open the heavy, creaking doors, revealing a sight that froze them in their tracks. The room was adorned with unholy symbols, and an oppressive aura of malevolence hung in the air. In the center of the chamber stood a figure, shrouded in darkness and surrounded by a legion of demonic entities.

The group leader, Mark, fought against the grip of fear threatening to paralyze him. He knew they had stumbled upon a more sinister force than they had ever imagined. Drawing upon his last reserves of strength, Mark reached deep within himself and summoned the only weapon he had left, faith.

With an unwavering voice, Mark cried out, "Jesus! Jesus! Jesus!" The room trembled, and a blinding light pierced the darkness. The demons recoiled, their hideous forms writhing in agony as the power of those sacred words washed over them.

One by one, the demons were banished, forced to retreat into the depths from which they had emerged. Their wails of anguish echoed through the chamber, filling the explorers' hearts with a mix of relief and awe. The oppressive atmosphere lifted, replaced by a sense of peace that had long been absent.

The explorers hurriedly left the chamber, trembling but emboldened by their victory. As they emerged into the moonlit night, they knew they had witnessed something beyond comprehension—a battle between the forces of light and darkness.

Word of their encounter spread throughout the land, and the forbidden chamber became known as a place forever tainted by the touch of evil. People spoke of the bravery of those who had faced the demons and the power of faith that had ultimately triumphed.

The explorers went their separate ways, forever changed by their harrowing experiences. They carried the knowledge that lurking in the shadows, there are forces both seen and unseen, and that sometimes, the power of belief and the invocation of the sacred can hold unimaginable strength.

And so, the legend of the forbidden chamber and the demons banished by the name of Jesus endured, a story whispered among those seeking to comprehend the boundaries between this world and the next.

Remember, it's just a spine-tingling tale, but it reminds us of the power of faith and the resilience of the human spirit. Happy Halloween!

The Devine Library

The Devine Library had always been a place of quiet contemplation and scholarly pursuit; its towering shelves filled with volumes on every subject imaginable. Lately, however, a palpable unease had settled over the grand old building, a sense that unseen eyes were watching the comings and goings of the students and faculty who passed through its doors.

It began with minor disturbances - books that would inexplicably fly off the shelves, lights flickering, the occasional whisper or strange noise that would send a shiver down one's spine. At first, the librarians and professors brushed it off as mere imagination, the product of tired minds and old buildings settling. But as the incidents escalated, a growing sense of dread took hold.

One evening, as the library was emptying out for the night, young Amelia, a second-year literature student, was gathering her things to leave. A book caught her eye as she descended the dimly lit stacks. It was lying open on a table, pages fluttering as if turned by an unseen hand. Amelia froze, her heart pounding. Slowly, she approached the table, the hairs on the back of her neck standing on end.

Just as she reached out to close the book, the lights suddenly flickered and went dark. Amelia let out a terrified yelp, fumbling in her bag for her phone. The glow of the screen illuminated the eerie scene - books were flying off the shelves, pages rustling and fluttering, as if caught in a whirlwind. Amelia backed away, her legs shaking, only to collide with something solid behind her.

She spun around, the phone's light revealing a figure's pale, gaunt face floating in midair. Amelia let out an agonized scream and fled, running headlong through the library, her footsteps echoing through the cavernous halls. She burst out the front doors, gasping for breath, her eyes wild with terror.

Word of the incident spread quickly, and soon, the Devine Library was the talk of the campus. Students and faculty alike whispered of the ghostly happenings, too afraid to venture inside after dark. Even during the day, an uneasy feeling hung in the air, as if the very walls of the building were imbued with a sinister energy.

Professor Eliza Winters, the head librarian, knew she couldn't let the rumors and fear continue to spiral. She convened a meeting with the university's dean and a team of parapsychologists, determined to get to the bottom of the haunting.

"We've had strange occurrences in the library before," Eliza explained, her brow furrowed with concern. "But nothing like this. Books flying off the shelves, unexplained noises, and now a student claiming to have seen a ghostly figure? We need to find out what's going on here."

The parapsychologists, a team of seasoned investigators, set to work, meticulously combing through the library and setting up an array of specialized equipment to monitor for any signs of paranormal activity. For days, they studied the library, taking readings and recordings, searching for clues that might shed light on the haunting.

The team began to piece together a disturbing story as the investigation progressed. Apparently, the Devine Library had a dark history, dating back to its construction in the late 19th century. The land on which it was built had once been the site of a small graveyard, and during the excavation, several unmarked graves had been uncovered and hastily relocated.

"It seems the library was built on top of those forgotten graves," one of the parapsychologists, a stern-faced woman named Dr. Simmons, reported. "And the spirits of those who were buried there may not have taken kindly to being disturbed."

Eliza's face paled at the revelation. "So, you're saying we've been desecrating a sacred site all this time? No wonder the library is haunted!"

Dr. Simmons nodded solemnly. "That's our working theory, at least. The energy of the site seems to have been disrupted, and the spirits of the dead are lashing out as a result."

The team's next step was to try to communicate with the restless spirits, to understand their grievances, and to find a way to appease them. They conducted séances and rituals for several nights, attempting to establish contact with the entities haunting the library.

The results were chilling. Voices whispered through the darkness, voices that seemed to come from everywhere and nowhere at once. They spoke of being wronged, of having their final resting place violated and desecrated. The team could feel the palpable anger and anguish emanating from the unseen presences.

"They want us to right the wrong that was done to them," Dr. Simmons announced, her face etched with a mixture of awe and trepidation. "They demand that we exhume their remains and give them a proper burial, or else they will continue to haunt this place forever."

Eliza felt a chill run down her spine. The thought of disturbing those graves again was deeply unsettling, but she knew they had no choice. The haunting had already escalated to a point where the safety of the students and faculty was at risk.

Something had to be done.

With a heavy heart, Eliza convened a meeting with the university's administration, laying out the team's findings and their proposed course of action. Despite the misgivings and concerns of some, it was ultimately decided that the graves would be exhumed and the remains reinterred in a proper cemetery.

The process was painstaking and emotionally fraught. As the excavation team carefully unearthed the forgotten graves, the air in the library grew thick with tension, and the disturbances intensified. Books flew off the shelves, lights flickered, and an eerie wailing could be heard echoing through the halls.

But the team pressed on, treating the recovered remains with the utmost care and respect. Once the exhumation was complete, they arranged for a solemn funeral procession, escorting the coffins to a nearby cemetery and laying the long-forgotten souls to rest.

As the final casket was lowered into the ground, a hush fell over the gathered crowd. For a moment, there was a palpable sense of stillness, as if the spirits themselves were finally at peace.

And indeed, the haunting of the Devine Library seemed to come to an end. The strange occurrences ceased, and a sense of calm and serenity returned to the grand old building. Eliza breathed a sigh of relief, grateful that the ordeal was finally over.

But even as the weeks and months passed, Eliza couldn't help but feel a lingering unease. She knew that the spirits had been wronged, their final resting place violated, and she couldn't help but wonder if the university had truly done enough to make amends.

Late one night, as Eliza was tidying up her office, she heard a faint whisper, barely audible, that sent a chill down her spine. "We will never forget..."

Eliza froze, her heart pounding. She glanced around the dimly lit office, half-expecting to see the ghostly figure she had heard so much about. But the room was empty, save for the flickering of the lamp on her desk.

Shaking her head, Eliza brushed off the unsettling feeling and headed home, determined to put the haunting behind her. But as she walked out of the library's front doors, she couldn't shake the nagging sense that the spirits of the Devine Library had not yet found the peace they so desperately sought.

The Haunted Firehouse

It was a dark and stormy night when the call came in - a fire had broken out at the old firehouse on the edge of town. The firefighters at Station 42 hurried to suit up and climb aboard the fire engine, the sirens wailing as they raced through the rain-soaked streets.

As they pulled up to the towering brick building, they could already see the orange glow of flames licking at the windows. "Alright, let's get in there and put this out!" shouted Captain Ramirez. The team sprang into action, dragging the hoses toward the entrance.

But as they approached the front doors, a sudden chill fell over them. The air seemed to grow thick and heavy, making it hard to breathe. Lieutenant Garcia paused, his hand gripping the door handle. "You guys feel that?" he said, his voice shaky.

"Come on, we don't have time for this!" yelled Ramirez. "The fire's spreading; we need to get in there!"

Swallowing hard, Garcia pushed open the door, and the team rushed inside. The lobby was dark, the emergency lights casting an eerie red glow over the scene—smoke billowed from the hallway leading to the garage, obscuring their vision.

"Thompson, Perez, you two take the hose and start attacking the fire. The rest of you fan out and make sure everyone's out of the building!" Ramirez commanded. The team split up, the thunderous sound of the fire engine's pump echoing through the halls.

As Perez and Thompson rounded the corner, they let out a terrified scream. A ghastly figure, shrouded in wispy black smoke, hovered just a few feet away. It seemed to glide effortlessly, its hollow eyes boring into them.

"What the hell is that?!" Thompson cried, stumbling backward. Perez didn't respond, frozen in terror. The ghostly apparition drifted closer, its skeletal hands reaching out towards them.

Snapping out of his paralysis, Thompson turned and ran, Perez close on his heels. "Captain, there's... there's something in here!" he yelled into his radio, his voice shaking. "Some kind of...ghost or something!"

Ramirez's voice crackled back through the static. "A ghost? Thompson, what are you talking about? Get back in there and put out that fire!"

"But sir, you don't understand! This thing, it's not human, it's -" Thompson's transmission cut out as he and Perez burst back into the lobby, nearly colliding with the rest of the team.

"Woah, what happened?" Garcia asked, grabbing Thompson's arm to steady him.

"There's... there's something in the hallway," Thompson panted. "Some kind of ghost or spirit or... I don't know what the hell it was, but it was not human!"

The others exchanged skeptical glances. "A ghost? Come on man, you're losing it," scoffed one of the firefighters.

"I'm telling you; I saw it! It was floating there, right in front of us!" Thompson insisted.

Ramirez strode over, his face stern. "Alright, that's enough. We've got a fire to put out, so let's stop with the ghost stories and get back to work. Thompson, Perez, get back in there and -"

Suddenly, a bone-chilling wail echoed through the building, causing everyone to jump. The lights flickered and dimmed, casting the lobby into an eerie shadow.

"What the...?" Ramirez whirled around, his eyes scanning the room. The other firefighters tensed, hands gripping their axes and hoses.

Another unearthly howl pierced the air, seeming to come from all around them. The lights continued to flicker, casting the room in a strobe-like effect.

"Alright, everyone stick together! We're getting out of here," Ramirez shouted, ushering his team towards the exit. But as they neared the door, it slammed shut with a resounding BANG, the lock turning by itself.

"What's happening?!" Garcia yelled, pulling futilely at the handle. The other firefighters rushed to the windows, only to find them locked as well,

the panes shuddering as if some unseen force was pressing against them.

Ramirez's radio crackled to life, the voice on the other end tinged with panic. "Captain, we can't get back in the building! The doors and windows are all sealed; we can't make entry!"

"Damn it!" Ramirez cursed, slamming his fist against the wall. "Alright, everyone stays calm. We're going to have to find another way out of here."

The team scattered, searching frantically for any sign of an exit. But as they explored the dark, smoky corridors, an overwhelming feeling of dread began to set in. The air grew thick and heavy, making it difficult to breathe. Strange sounds echoed around them - creaking floorboards, the faint patter of unseen footsteps, and that chilling, unearthly wail that seemed to reverberate through their very bones.

Rounding a corner, Perez let out a terrified scream. There, hovering just a few feet away, was the ghostly figure they had seen earlier. It drifted closer, its empty eye sockets boring into them, and a sense of pure terror gripped the firefighters.

"Run!" Ramirez shouted, and the team fled down the hall, the spectral being in pursuit. They could hear it howling behind them, the sound growing ever closer. Smoke and shadows seemed to swirl around them, obscuring their vision and making it hard to tell which way they were going.

Suddenly, Garcia stumbled and fell, his ankle twisted at an unnatural angle. "Ahhh!" he cried out in pain, struggling to get back to his feet.

"Garcia! Come on, we've gotta keep moving!" Thompson yelled, grabbing his arm and trying to pull him up.

But Garcia shook his head, his face etched with fear. "I can't... it's too late for me. Just go, save yourselves!"

The ghostly figure was closing in, its unearthly wail filling the air. The other firefighters hesitated, torn between leaving their comrade and fleeing to safety.

"Go, damn it!" Garcia shouted, shoving Thompson away. With a deep breath, he turned to face the approaching specter, his hand gripping his axe in a white-knuckled grip.

The others reluctantly obeyed, running down the smoke-filled hall as fast as they could. They could hear Garcia's desperate shouts and the crash of his axe against the supernatural entity, followed by a final, agonizing scream that made their blood run cold.

Ramirez led the way, his mind racing. "There's got to be another way out of here. We can't be trapped; there has to be -" He froze as they rounded a corner, the color draining from his face.

Blocking their path was another ghastly figure, its skeletal limbs floating just above the floor. It regarded them with hollow, glowing eyes, a sinister aura emanating from its very being.

The firefighters scrambled to turn back, but the way was blocked by a swirling mass of black smoke. They were surrounded, trapped like rats in a maze.

Ramirez gripped his radio, his voice shaking. "Dispatch, this is Captain Ramirez. We're trapped inside the firehouse, the doors and windows are sealed, and... and there's some kind of... supernatural entity here. We need immediate backup and extraction... Over!"

Static crackled in response. "Copy that, Station 42. We're mobilizing all available units, but the roads are impassable due to the storm. ETA unknown, over."

Ramirez swore under his breath, his heart pounding in his chest. He turned to his remaining team, their faces etched with terror. "Alright, listen up. We're going to have to fight our way out of this. Stick together, and don't let that... thing get near you, understand?"

The others nodded shakily, gripping their axes and hoses. Ramirez took a deep breath and stepped forward, praying that somehow, someway, they would make it out of this nightmare alive.

As the ghostly figure advanced, the firefighters braced themselves for the fight of their lives.

The ghostly figure advanced menacingly, its skeletal hands reaching out towards the firefighters. Ramirez raised his axe, his knuckles white with tension.

"Alright team, stick together and hit it with everything you've got!" he yelled. The others rushed forward, water from their hoses spraying in all directions.

But as the water hit the specter, it simply passed through its ethereal form, having no effect. The figure continued its slow, deliberate advance, its hollow eyes burning with malice.

"What the...?" Thompson's voice was tinged with panic. "Nothing's working! How are we supposed to stop this thing?"

Ramirez gritted his teeth, his mind racing. "I don't know, but we have to try! Keep hammering away at it!"

The firefighters continued their assault, swinging their axes and dousing the apparition with water. But their efforts were in vain - the ghostly being seemed impervious to their attacks, barely slowing its approach.

Suddenly, a bone-chilling wail echoed through the hall, and the smoky air around them began to swirl and churn. More spectral figures emerged from the darkness, their translucent bodies drifting closer.

"Oh god, there's more of them!" Perez cried, his voice cracking with terror. The firefighters huddled together, their backs to the wall as the ghosts surrounded them.

Ramirez's mind raced, desperately searching for a way out. "Alright, we can't fight these things head-on. We need to find another way - a way to escape this hellhole!"

He scanned the corridor, his eyes landing on a partially-opened door at the far end. "There! That way, quickly!"

The team made a mad dash for the door, the spectral figures closing in behind them. As they reached the threshold, Ramirez paused, ushering the others through.

"Go, go! I'll hold them off!" he shouted, swinging his axe wildly at the approaching ghosts. The others hesitated, but Ramirez pushed them forward. "That's an order! Now get the hell out of here!"

Reluctantly, the firefighters scrambled through the door, slamming it shut behind them. Ramirez braced himself against it, his heart pounding, as the unearthly wails of the ghosts filled the air.

On the other side, the remaining firefighters found themselves in a small room – a kitchen, by the looks of it. They huddled together, their faces etched with fear and uncertainty.

"What do we do now?" Perez whispered, his voice trembling. "We're trapped in here, and the captain..."

Thompson placed a hand on his shoulder, his own expression grim. "We have to keep moving. There has to be another way out of this place."

They moved cautiously through the kitchen, searching for another exit. But as they explored the room, an unsettling feeling began to creep over them. The air felt thick and heavy, and the shadows seemed to shift and dance as if alive.

Suddenly, a high-pitched giggle echoed from the far corner of the kitchen, causing them all to freeze. Slowly, they turned to face the source of the sound, their hearts pounding in their chests.

In the dimly lit corner sat a small, spectral figure – a child, its translucent body floating inches above the floor. It regarded them with eerie, glowing eyes, a twisted smile stretching across its face.

The firefighters stood, transfixed by the sight, as the ghostly child drifted towards them, its laughter growing louder and more menacing with each passing moment.

As the ghostly child drifted closer, the firefighters found themselves frozen in place, their bodies gripped by a deep, primal fear.

Thompson's voice quavered as he spoke up, trying to reason with the apparition. "H-hey there, little one. We don't want any trouble. We're just trying to find a way out of here. Can you help us?"

The child tilted its head to the side, the twisted smile never leaving its face. Then, in a high-pitched, sing-song voice, it replied, "Ohhh, but I don't want you to leave. I want you to stay and play with me..."

The firefighters exchanged uneasy glances, their muscles tensing as the child drew closer. Perez's hand gripped the hose, his knuckles turning white.

"I don't think this is a good idea," he murmured. "We need to get out of here, now."

But before they could make a move, the child let out a shrill cackle and extended a bony, translucent hand towards them. Suddenly, a wave of icy energy washed over the firefighters, causing them to stagger and gasp in shock.

"What the…." Thompson choked, his breath visible in the suddenly frigid air. The child's eyes gleamed with malicious delight as it continued its advance.

"Yes, stay and play with me…" it hissed, its voice reverberating through the room. "I've been so lonely, and you all look like such fun new friends…"

The firefighters huddled together, their minds racing as they tried to think of a way to escape the child's icy grasp. Perez's grip on the hose tightened, and he met the eyes of his teammates, a steely determination etched on his face.

"We're not going to be your playthings, you little creep," he growled. "If you want a fight, you've got one."

With that, he swung the hose towards the child, the powerful stream of water slamming into its ethereal form. The child let out a shriek of pain and surprise, its body flickering and distorting as the water struck it.

The other firefighters quickly followed suit, unleashing a barrage of water and swinging their axes at the spectral figure. The child thrashed and wailed, its icy grip on the room faltering as it struggled against their onslaught.

"Keep it up!" Thompson yelled, his voice strained with exertion. "We've got to drive this thing out of here!"

The battle raged on, the firefighters' combined efforts slowly forcing the ghostly child back, its cries of anguish echoing through the kitchen. But as they pushed it toward the corner, a new, unsettling realization dawned on them.

The shadows in the room were shifting and gathering, coalescing into a larger, more menacing presence. A deep, bone-chilling growl rumbled through the air, and the firefighters felt their blood run cold.

They had sensed the child's malevolence, but this new force... it was something far darker, far more ancient and powerful. And it was closing in, ready to join the fray.

The firefighters froze, their bodies tensing as the deep, bone-chilling growl reverberated through the kitchen. They exchanged panicked glances, realizing they were now facing an even greater threat than the ghostly child.

"What the hell was that?" Perez whispered, his voice barely audible. "Please tell me I'm just imagining things..."

Thompson shook his head, his eyes wide with fear. "No, I heard it too. And it's not alone – look at the shadows!"

The firefighters turned their focus to the corners of the room, where the shadows seemed to be gathering and swirling. A sense of dread crept up their spines as they watched the dark tendrils coalesce, forming a towering, and amorphous shape.

Suddenly, a pair of glowing, crimson eyes emerged from the darkness, piercing through the gloom. A deep, rumbling growl emanated from the shadowy figure, sending shivers down the firefighters' spines.

"Oh god, we're trapped," Perez breathed, his grip on the hose trembling. "There's no way we can fight something like that."

Thompson swallowed hard, his mind racing for a solution. "Alright, listen up. We need to get out of this room, now. That thing is our priority – we can't waste time dealing with the kid."

He turned to the others, his expression grim but determined. "Stick together, and move fast. We might have a chance if we can make it to the door. But we've got to move, _now_."

Without hesitation, the firefighters began to retreat from the advancing shadow, their hoses still trained on the ghostly child. Perez and Thompson took the lead, while the others followed closely behind, their eyes darting nervously toward the looming, crimson-eyed presence.

As they neared the kitchen door, the shadow let out another bone-chilling growl, its form swelling and pulsing menacingly. The ghostly child, now dazed and weakened from their assault, hissed and lunged towards them, its clawed hands reaching out.

"Come on, come on!" Thompson yelled, his voice laced with panic. "We're so close, just keep moving!"

The firefighters pushed through the door, slamming it shut behind them and barricading it with whatever they could find. They could hear the furious, unearthly cries of the child and the deep, rumbling growls of the shadowy presence on the other side, but they dared not stop.

Gasping for breath, they turned to face the dimly lit hallway, their minds racing as they tried to determine their next move. The air was thick with tension, and they could feel the weight of the supernatural forces closing in around them.

"Alright, guys," Ramirez's voice suddenly rang out from the darkness, causing them to jump in surprise. "I don't know what the hell is going on, but we need to keep moving. There has to be a way out of this hellhole."

The firefighters whirled around to see their captain, battered and bruised but alive, emerging from the shadows. Relief and hope flickered across their faces, but a renewed sense of determination quickly replaced it.

"Captain, you made it!" Perez exclaimed. "But we've got bigger problems now. There's some kind of... *thing* in there, and it's not alone."

Ramirez's expression darkened as he listened to their account, his jaw tightening with resolve. "Then we don't have a moment to lose. Let's move – and keep your eyes peeled. We don't know what else might be waiting for us in the dark."

With that, the team of firefighters steeled themselves and pressed on, their hearts racing as they ventured deeper into the haunted firehouse, determined to find a way to escape the supernatural horrors that lurked within.

As the firefighters cautiously made their way through the dimly lit hallway, their senses were on high alert, searching for any potential clues or means of escape.

Perez, who was leading the way, suddenly paused, his brow furrowed in concentration. "Wait, do you guys hear that?" he whispered.

The others strained their ears, and soon they too could make out the faint sound of... running water? It was coming from somewhere up ahead, growing louder as they drew closer.

"A water source," Thompson murmured, his eyes widening with hope. "Maybe we can use it to our advantage against those... *things* back there."

Ramirez nodded, his expression grim but determined. "Good catch, Perez. Let's see where it's coming from."

They pressed on, their footsteps muffled by the worn carpet as they followed the sound of rushing water. Turning a corner, they came upon a small utility room, the source of the noise – a leaking pipe, its steady drip echoing in the stillness.

"This could work," Ramirez said, surveying the room. "Alright, everyone, spread out and see if you can find anything else useful in here."

The firefighters quickly got to work, scouring the room for tools, equipment, or anything that could aid their escape. Perez, in the far corner, suddenly let out a triumphant cry.

"Guys, I found it! There's an emergency exit right here!"

The others rushed over, their hearts pounding with renewed hope. Sure enough, a heavy metal door was partially obscured by a stack of boxes, leading to what appeared to be the outside.

"Thank god," Thompson breathed, his shoulders sagging with relief. "Okay, let's get this door open and-"

But before he could finish, a thunderous crash echoed from the hallway, followed by the unmistakable sound of the kitchen door being torn from its hinges. The firefighters froze, their blood running cold as they listened to the deep, rumbling growl that reverberated through the air.

"It's coming," Ramirez whispered, his face pale. "We need to move *now*."

Perez and Thompson quickly began clearing the boxes away from the emergency exit, their hands trembling. Ramirez and the others took up defensive positions, their hoses and axes at the ready, bracing themselves for the impending confrontation.

The sound of the approaching shadow grew louder; its presence felt like a physical weight in the air. The firefighters could almost feel the evil energy radiating towards them, sending shivers down their spines.

As the towering, shadowy figure emerged in the doorway, its crimson eyes glowing with unholy power, the firefighters knew that their only hope of survival lay in reaching that emergency exit – and they were running out of time.

The firefighters knew they had to act quickly and quietly if they wanted to escape the looming creature through the emergency exit. Perez and Thompson continued clearing the boxes away, making as little noise as possible.

"Ramirez, can you distract that thing somehow?" Perez whispered urgently. "We need a few more seconds to get this door open."

Ramirez's brow furrowed as he considered their options. "I might be able to," he replied, his voice low. "But it's risky. That... *thing* doesn't seem like it's going to be easily fooled."

The captain glanced back at the shadowy figure, which was now slowly advancing into the room, its crimson eyes fixed on the firefighters. He had to think fast.

"Alright, listen up," Ramirez said, turning to the others. "Thompson, Perez, keep working on that door. The rest of you, spread out and get ready to hit that creature with everything we've got. I'm going to try and draw its attention."

The firefighters nodded, their faces tense with determination. Ramirez took a deep breath, then stepped forward, raising his ax and shouting.

"Hey, ugly! Over here!"

The creature's head snapped towards Ramirez, its growl deepening as it focused on the captain. Ramirez held his ground, swinging his ax in a menacing arc.

"Come and get me, you bastard!" he yelled, his voice echoing through the room.

The creature responded with a bone-chilling roar, its massive form surging forward. Ramirez backpedaled, luring the creature away from the emergency exit as the others fired their hoses, dousing it with streams of water.

Perez and Thompson worked frantically, their fingers fumbling with the latch on the heavy metal door. "Come on, come on," Perez muttered under his breath, his brow furrowed in concentration.

Finally, with a loud click, the latch gave way, and the door swung open. "Got it!" Thompson shouted, his voice laced with relief.

"Everyone, through the door, *now*!" Ramirez bellowed, his ax swinging to keep the creature at bay.

The firefighters didn't need to be told twice. They rushed through the open doorway one by one, splashing through a shallow puddle and out into the cool night air. Perez and Thompson were the last to exit, slipping through the door and slamming it shut behind them.

After the firefighters managed to open the emergency exit and flee the firehouse, they were able to get to safety. The unearthly creatures that had been terrorizing them remained trapped inside the building.

In the days that followed, the abandoned firehouse seemed to take on an ominous air, with locals reporting strange noises and sightings around the old structure. Some chalked it up to their imagination or stray wildlife, but the firefighters who had experienced the horrors firsthand knew the truth.

Eventually, the decision was made to demolish the firehouse entirely. Perhaps the authorities wanted to put an end to the unsettling rumors and urban legends surrounding the place. Or maybe they simply couldn't risk leaving such a potentially dangerous building standing.

Regardless, within a week of the firefighters' harrowing ordeal, the old firehouse was reduced to rubble. The only ones who truly knew what had transpired there were the brave firefighters who had barely escaped with their lives.

The fate of the unearthly creatures that had been imprisoned inside remained a mystery. Had they been destroyed in the demolition, or had they found another way to escape? It was a question that would haunt the minds of those who had witnessed the firefighters' brush with the unknown.

In the end, the old firehouse and its dark secrets were erased, leaving only whispers and speculation in its wake. But for the firefighters involved, the memory of that fateful day would never truly fade away.

The Haunted Jack-O-Lantern

It was a chilly Halloween night. Mike and his little sister Sandy were out trick-or-treating in their neighborhood, their costumes glowing under the streetlights. As they approached one particularly spooky-looking house, Sandy noticed an old, gnarled pumpkin sitting on the porch steps.

"Look, Mike! That jack-o'-lantern looks really creepy," Sandy whispered, eyeing the pumpkin warily. Its jagged teeth and menacing expression seemed to be glaring right at them.

Mike laughed. "Aw, it's probably just some old decoration. Come on, let's go get some more candy!"

Sandy couldn't shake the feeling that the pumpkin was watching them as they walked up to the front door. When they returned to the porch a few minutes later, the jack-o'-lantern's expression seemed to have changed - the carved eyes were narrowed, and the mouth curled into a sinister grin.

"Mike, I really don't like that pumpkin," Sandy said, tugging on her brother's sleeve. "Can we just go?"

"Relax, it's just a dumb pumpkin," Mike scoffed. "It can't hurt us."

But as they turned to leave, a strange orange glow began to emanate from the jack-o'-lantern. Suddenly, the pumpkin let out an unearthly cackle that frightened both children.

To their horror, the jack-o'-lantern's face seemed to melt and reform, twisting into an even more menacing visage. Glowing embers flickered deep within its hollow eyes and mouth.

"Run, Sandy, run!" Mike yelled, grabbing his sister's hand and sprinting down the sidewalk as fast as they could. Behind them, the haunted pumpkin let out another bone-chilling laugh that echoed through the streets.

The terrified siblings didn't stop running until they reached the safety of their own home, vowing never to go near that spooky jack-o'-lantern again.

The Haunting at Hollow's Edge

The old Blackwood mansion had always been the talk of the town. Looming ominously at the edge of Hollow's Edge, the dilapidated estate was cloaked in an air of mystery and dread. Locals whispered rumors that the place was haunted, and unearthly howls and bloodcurdling screams could be heard from its crumbling walls on Halloween night.

Most people steered clear of the Blackwood mansion, giving it a wide berth as they hurried past, their eyes averted. But on this particular All Hallows' Eve, a group of local teenagers were determined to uncover the truth behind the ghostly legends.

It was nearing midnight when the group of five - Sam, Chloe, Ethan, Addy, and Dylan - gathered at the edge of the Blackwood property, their breath visible in the chilly autumn air.

"Are you sure about this?" Addy asked nervously, wrapping her coat tighter around herself. "I have a really bad feeling..."

"Don't be such a wimp, Addy," Ethan scoffed. "This is our chance to finally put the Blackwood ghost stories to rest. Think about the bragging rights!"

Chloe rolled her eyes. "Ethan's right; this is our opportunity to make history. No more silly rumors - we're going to be the ones to uncover the truth."

Sam and Dylan exchanged a worried glance, but ultimately agreed to go along with the plan. The group steeled their nerves and began making their way up the long, overgrown driveway toward the mansion.

An eerie silence fell over the property as they approached the imposing wrought-iron gates. The usual sounds of nocturnal wildlife were strangely absent, leaving an unsettling quiet in their wake. Chloe raised a shaky hand and pushed open the creaking gates, leading the group inside. The Blackwood mansion loomed before them, its once-grand facade crumbling and decrepit. Ivy snaked up the sides of the building, and several of the windows were broken, their jagged glass glinting in the moonlight. An uneasy feeling settled in the pit of Sam's stomach as they made their way up the front steps and toward the sagging front door.

"Maybe we should just go back," he murmured. "This doesn't feel right."

"Don't be such a baby," Dylan scoffed, giving Sam a rough shove forward. "Let's just get this over with."

Steeling themselves, the group slowly pushed open the heavy oak door and stepped inside. The entryway was pitch black, the only illumination from the thin slivers of moonlight filtering through the grimy windows. An oppressive silence hung in the air, broken only by the sound of their own nervous feet.

As the teenagers stepped into the Blackwood mansion's dark entryway, a chill ran down their spines. The air was thick with an unsettling stillness; the only sound was the creaking of the old floorboards beneath their feet.

"I don't like this," Addy whispered, her voice shaking. "We should get out of here."

Ethan scoffed. "Don't be such a wimp. Where's your sense of adventure?" He reached into his backpack and pulled out a large flashlight, clicking it on and sweeping the beam of light across the shadowy space.

The entryway was in a state of disrepair, with dust and cobwebs coating every surface. An ornate chandelier hung overhead, its crystal prisms caked with grime. A grand staircase led up to the second floor, the wooden steps warped and groaning under the weight of the teenagers' footsteps.

"This place is a dump," Chloe remarked, wrinkling her nose in disgust. "Let's just find whatever's supposed to be haunting this place and get it over with."

The group cautiously moved further into the mansion, Ethan's flashlight illuminating their path. As they passed through a set of double doors, they entered what appeared to be a once-grand living room. Tattered curtains hung lifelessly at the windows, and an overturned sofa lay on its side, springs poking through the shredded upholstery.

"Woah," Dylan breathed, stepping over a broken end table. "This place is really falling apart."

Sam trailed behind the others, his eyes darting nervously around the room. "I really think we should leave. There's something... off about this place."

Chloe shot him an exasperated look. "Oh, come on, Sam. Don't ruin this for everyone. We're so close to solving the mystery of the Blackwood mansion!" She turned and continued on, the others following suit.

The group descended a long, shadowy hallway; Ethan's flashlight flickered slightly, casting unnerving shadows on the peeling wallpaper.

"The basement," Chloe suddenly announced, pointing to a set of wooden stairs leading down. "That's where we'll find the answers."

Without hesitation, she began descending the stairs, the others trailing behind her. The basement was cloaked in near-total darkness, save for the wavering beam of Ethan's flashlight. As they reached the bottom, Sam felt a wave of dread wash over him.

"Guys, I really don't think we should be down here," he protested weakly. "This is a bad idea."

Addy nodded in agreement. "Sam's right. I have a terrible feeling about this."

Ethan rolled his eyes. "You two are such killjoys. If you're too scared, you can wait up here." He turned and continued on, the others reluctantly following.

The basement was a maze of shadowy corridors and crumbling, abandoned rooms. Debris and rubble littered the floor, and the air had a musty, oppressive quality to it. As they ventured deeper underground, the group couldn't shake the sense that they were being watched. Suddenly, Chloe let out a small gasp.

"Look, over there!" She pointed the flashlight toward a doorway, its frame partially obscured by a collapsed support beam.

The others followed her gaze, their breath catching in their throats. Beyond the doorway, a flickering light could be seen, casting an eerie glow.

"What is that?" Addy whispered, clutching Chloe's arm.

Ethan grinned, his eyes gleaming with excitement. "Only one way to find out." He began making his way toward the doorway, the others reluctantly trailing behind.

As they approached the room, an unsettling feeling of dread grew stronger with each step. The air seemed to grow colder, and the silence was deafening. Steeling their nerves, the group stepped through the threshold and into the room beyond.

It was a small, cramped space, the walls lined with ancient, rusting shelves. The flickering light came from a single, guttering candle situated on a rickety table in the center of the room. Ethan swept the flashlight around, illuminating the strange objects that filled the shelves - jars filled with what appeared to be preserved organs, dusty tomes with occult symbols etched into their spines, and an array of arcane-looking tools and instruments.

"What is this place?" Chloe murmured, her eyes wide with a mixture of fascination and horror.

"It looks like some kind of... occult laboratory," Addy replied shakily. "We need to get out of here. Now."

But before anyone could move, a sudden noise made them all freeze. A low, guttural growl seemed to emanate from the shadows in the room's far corner. The group spun around, Ethan's flashlight trembling in his hand as he swept it toward the sound.

What emerged from the darkness made their blood run cold. Shrouded in a tattered, dark cloak, a large, hulking figure slowly rose to its full height. Glowing, red eyes pierced through the gloom, fixed on the terrified teenagers.

"What the hell is that?" Dylan breathed, his voice barely above a whisper.

The creature let out an unearthly howl, the sound sending shivers down the group's spines. It began lumbering toward them, its clawed hands reaching out menacingly.

"Run!" Chloe screamed, already turning and sprinting toward the doorway. The others didn't need to be told twice, and they bolted after her, their footsteps echoing through the shadowy corridors of the basement.

The group raced up the creaking stairs, their hearts pounding in their chests. They could hear the creature's heavy footsteps thundering behind them, its guttural snarls growing louder with each passing moment.

"Hurry!" Ethan yelled, his voice laced with panic. "We've gotta get out of here!"

They burst out of the basement and back into the dark, dilapidated mansion, the creature in hot pursuit. Addy let out a terrified shriek as one of its clawed hands swiped at her, barely missing her shoulder. The group barreled through the living room, knocking over furniture in their haste to escape.

Finally, they reached the front door and flung it open, spilling out onto the overgrown lawn. They didn't stop running until they reached the safety of the old iron gates, their chests heaving and their faces pale with terror.

"What the hell was that thing?" Dylan gasped, his eyes wide with shock.

Chloe shook her head, trembling. "I don't know, but we need to get out of here. Now."

The group hurried down the long driveway, not daring to look back. They didn't stop until they reached the main road, their footsteps pounding against the asphalt.

Once they were a safe distance away, they finally allowed themselves to catch their breath. Addy was shaking uncontrollably, tears streaming down her face.

"I told you we shouldn't have gone in there," she sobbed. "I had a bad feeling, and now we've seen... that thing."

Ethan ran a hand through his hair, his bravado gone. "Yeah, well, you were right. That was... that was not what I was expecting."

Sam wrapped an arm around Addy, trying to calm her. "We need to tell someone. The police, or the town council, or... someone. That thing is still in there, and it's dangerous."

Chloe nodded, her expression grave. "You're right. We can't just keep this to ourselves. Who knows what else is lurking in that place?"

The group made their way to the local police station, their voices shaking as they recounted the harrowing ordeal. The officers listened with growing concern, their faces paling as the teenagers described the horrific creature they had encountered.

"You're certain it wasn't just some kind of wild animal?" one officer asked skeptically.

Ethan shook his head emphatically. "No way, man. That thing... it wasn't human. It was like something out of a nightmare."

The police promised to investigate the matter, dispatching a team to the Blackwood mansion immediately. The teenagers were advised to stay away from the property for their own safety until the situation was resolved.

As the group parted ways, a heavy silence fell over them. The haunting at Hollow's Edge had become all too real, and they couldn't escape the lingering dread that had settled in their stomachs.

What kind of dark, unspeakable evil had they uncovered in the depths of the Blackwood mansion? And would the police be able to stop it before it was too late?

The Haunting of Colonial Williamsburg

It was a cool autumn night in 1775 as Thomas Randolph made his way down the dimly lit streets of Williamsburg. The young lawyer had been working late at the colonial capitol building, poring over legal documents by the flickering light of a candle.

A strange sense of unease crept over him as he hurried back to his modest lodgings. The shadows seemed to shift and move in the corners of his vision, and he could have sworn he heard the faint sound of footsteps following behind him.

Picking up his pace, Thomas quickened his steps, his heart pounding in his chest. Just as he reached the end of the street, a sudden gust of wind whipped through the air, extinguishing the lantern he carried. Thomas was plunged into darkness.

He froze, straining his eyes to make out any shapes in the gloom. That's when he saw a pale, ghostly figure drifting towards him, its features obscured but its presence unmistakable. Thomas let out a cry of terror and began to run, his boots pounding against the cobblestones.

He didn't stop until he reached the safety of his boarding house, bursting through the door and slamming it behind him. The landlady, awakened by the commotion, came hurrying down the stairs.

"Good heavens, Mr. Randolph, whatever is the matter?" she exclaimed.

Thomas, trembling, recounted his eerie encounter on the street. The landlady listened, her eyes widening.

"Why, that sounds like the ghost of Lady Skipwith!" she whispered. "They say her spirit still wanders the streets of Williamsburg, forever searching for her lost love."

From that night on, Thomas avoided venturing out after dark, his mind haunted by the vision of the ghostly Lady Skipwith. The true haunting of colonial Williamsburg had begun.

The Rock Monster's Halloween Adventure

It was a spooky Halloween night in the forest. All the animals were getting ready to go trick-or-treating. All except one - the big, grumpy rock monster.

The rock monster lived under a huge boulder near the creek. He didn't like Halloween at all. He thought the costumes were silly and the candy was too sweet. All he wanted to do was stay in his cave and be left alone.

The rock monster grumbled and groaned as the other animals walked by, dressed up in their costumes. "Bah, humbug!" he would shout. "Get off my lawn!"

But one little girl dressed like a fairy princess heard the rock monster grumble. She decided she would try to make the rock monster feel better.

"Hello, Mr. Rock Monster!" said the fairy princess. "Why aren't you out trick-or-treating with everyone else?"

"Bah!" said the rock monster. "Halloween is stupid. I don't want any part of it."

The fairy princess thought for a moment. "Well, would you like to come trick-or-treating with me?" she asked. "I have lots of extra candy I could share with you."

The rock monster was surprised. No one had ever invited him to go trick-or-treating before. "You... you want me to come with you?" he asked.

"Of course!" said the fairy princess. "It's more fun with friends!"

The rock monster thought about it for a moment. Maybe Halloween wouldn't be so bad if he had a friend to share it with. "Alright," he grumbled. "I'll give it a try."

And so the rock monster and the fairy princess set off together, going from house to house and collecting all sorts of yummy Halloween treats. The rock monster was still a little grumpy, but he had to admit - it was kind of fun.

By the end of the night, the rock monster's heart had grown three sizes. He realized that Halloween wasn't so bad after all, especially when you had a good friend by your side. From that day on, the rock monster looked forward to Halloween every year, ready to go trick-or-treating with his new fairy princess friend.

The Witches' Chant

A chill would creep down my spine every Halloween as the twilight faded into night. Growing up in the rural countryside of Missouri, our little farmhouse stood alone, surrounded by fields of swaying corn and the dark, looming shadows of the old oak trees.

As the sun dipped below the horizon, the air would grow still and heavy, as if the very land itself held its breath in anticipation. And then, faint at first, I would hear it - a haunting, lilting chant drifting on the breeze.

"Help me, help me, the spirits call..." The words seemed to float all around, emanating from the dense forest that bordered our property. My heart would pound as I strained to hear more, my imagination running wild with thoughts of dark rituals and unearthly beings.

The chanting would grow louder, the voices blending together in an eerie, otherworldly melody. "Help me, help me, the moon is high..."

I knew I shouldn't go investigate and stay safe inside. But the allure of the unknown was too strong. Slowly, tentatively, I would make my way through the fields, toward the tree line, drawn by the primal power of the chant.

As I approached the forest's edge, the chanting would suddenly fall silent, leaving an unnerving quiet in its wake. I would peer into the blackness between the twisted, gnarled trees, searching for any sign of movement, any glimpse of the mysterious chanters.

But there was nothing, only the rustling of leaves and the hoot of an owl in the distance. Shivering, I would quickly turn back, hurrying to the safety of the house, my mind racing with questions.

Who were those chanting voices? What dark rituals were they performing deep in the woods? And would I ever discover the truth behind the haunting Halloween chant?

October 31st, 1966

The cool autumn breeze rustled the bare branches of the trees as I made my way across the field, my heart pounding with a mix of fear and anticipation. It was Halloween night, and once again, I could hear the eerie chanting drifting through the air, beckoning me to venture into the shadowy forest.

I had heard the haunting voices every year since I was a child, but this year was different. I was 18 now, no longer a frightened little girl. I was determined to uncover the mystery once and for all.

As I reached the edge of the trees, the chanting grew louder, the words echoing all around me. "Help me, help me, the spirits call..." I took a deep breath and stepped into the darkness, my footsteps crunching on the fallen leaves.

The forest was thick and dense, the gnarled branches forming a tangled canopy overhead that blocked out the moonlight. I stumbled through the underbrush, following the sound of the chanting, my eyes straining to make out any shapes in the inky blackness. Suddenly, a flickering light appeared up ahead, and the chanting grew even louder. I crept forward cautiously, my breath catching in my throat as I glimpsed the source of the light - a small clearing, where a group of hooded figures stood in a circle, their voices raised in an eerie incantation.

I ducked behind a large tree trunk, peering out at the scene unfolding before me. The figures were swaying back and forth, their hands clasped together as they chanted in unison—a fire burned in the center of the circle, casting an otherworldly glow over the proceedings. My mind raced as I tried to make sense of what I was seeing. Were these really witches, performing some kind of dark ritual in the dead of night? The thought both terrified and fascinated me.

As I watched, the chanting reached a crescendo, the figures raising their arms to the sky. Then, one by one, they began to remove their hoods, revealing the faces of... my neighbors?

I stifled a gasp as I recognized the familiar features of the town mayor, the local schoolteacher, and several other prominent members of the community.

What were they doing out here, under the cloak of darkness, engaging in what appeared to be some kind of occult ceremony?

The figures began to move around the fire, their chanting shifting into a rhythmic, pulsing beat. Suddenly, one of them broke away from the circle, her long, dark hair flowing behind her as she danced around the flames, her movements wild and graceful.

I watched, transfixed, as the woman swayed and twirled, her body moving in perfect sync with the chanting of the others. There was an almost primal energy to her movements, a raw, elemental power that captivated me.

As the dance reached its climax, the figures began to slowly disperse, their chanting fading into the night.

I remained hidden, my heart pounding, as the last of the hooded figures disappeared into the trees, leaving the clearing empty save for the dying embers of the fire. Cautiously, I stepped out from my hiding place, my mind racing with questions. What had I just witnessed? Were these people really practicing some kind of witchcraft, right here in our small, seemingly ordinary town?

I knew that I should go back home, that I should forget what I had seen and never speak of it again. But I couldn't shake the nagging sense of curiosity and unease that had taken hold of me. I had to know more. Especially since one was my own sister. How could this be? Surely not. This alone will haunt me to my dying days.

Trick or Treat

It was a dark and spooky Halloween night. The moon was full, the wind was howling, and the trees were casting eerie shadows across the neighborhood streets.

Little Timmy was so excited to go trick-or-treating. For months, he had been planning his superhero costume - a bright red cape, a mask with pointy ears, and shiny silver boots. Timmy's best friends, Sarah and Jared, were going trick-or-treating with him. Sarah was dressed as a beautiful princess, and Jared was a creepy-looking vampire.

The three friends set out down the sidewalk, their bags and buckets empty and ready to be filled with delicious Halloween candy.

They walked past house after house, ringing doorbells and yelling "Trick-or-treat!"

The neighbors were so impressed by their creative costumes, and they showered the kids with handfuls of chocolates, lollipops, and other sugary treats.

After a while, Timmy noticed a strange-looking house down at the end of the block. It was old and run-down, with peeling paint on the walls and a giant, twisted tree in the front yard. The tree's branches stretched up toward the night sky, casting long, spooky shadows across the lawn.

"Hey guys, let's go to that house next!" Timmy said excitedly, pointing down the street.

Sarah and Jared exchanged nervous glances. "I don't know, Timmy. That house looks really creepy. Are you sure we should go there?"

But Timmy was determined. "Come on, it'll be fun! Maybe they have the best candy!" He grabbed his friends' hands and began pulling them down the sidewalk.

As they got closer to the old house, Timmy could feel his heart start to beat a little faster. There was something ominous about it, something that sent a shiver down his spine. But Timmy pushed those feelings aside. He was a superhero, and superheroes weren't afraid of anything!

When they reached the front door, Timmy took a deep breath and rang the doorbell. *DING DONG!* The door slowly creaked open, and Timmy peered inside, expecting to see a scary witch or a howling monster.

But instead, out popped a little orange cat! "Meow!" it said, blinking its big green eyes at the three trick-or-treaters.

Timmy, Sarah, and Jared burst out laughing. The cat just sat there, looking up at them with a confused expression.

"I guess this house isn't so scary after all!" Timmy giggled. He held out his bag, and the cat sniffed it curiously. "Trick-or-treat, little kitty!"

The cat meowed again and then scurried back inside, disappearing into the darkness of the old house.

The three friends gathered their candy and continued on their way, laughing and talking about the silly orange cat the whole time.

Timmy started to notice other strange things about the neighborhood as they walked. The trees seemed to be moving independently, their branches reaching out toward the kids. And was that a pair of glowing eyes he saw peeking out from behind a bush?

"Hey guys, did you see that?" Timmy whispered, his eyes wide with excitement.

Sarah shook her head. "See what?"

"I thought I saw something in the bushes over there. And the trees look like they're reaching for us!"

Jared laughed. "You're just being silly, Timmy. It's probably just the wind making the trees move."

But Timmy wasn't so sure. He kept glancing around nervously, half-expecting to see a monster or a ghost jump out at them from the shadows.

As they approached the next house, Timmy noticed something else strange. The porch light was flickering on and off, casting an eerie glow over the front yard.

"Guys, look at that!" Timmy exclaimed, pointing at the flashing light.

Sarah frowned. "That is kind of weird. Maybe the bulb is going out?"

Timmy shook his head. "I don't know, you guys. This whole neighborhood is starting to feel really spooky."

Just then, a loud THUMP came from somewhere behind them, making all three kids jump in fright.

"What was that?!" Jared cried, his vampire fangs chattering.

Timmy's heart was racing. "I-I don't know. Let's just hurry up and get to the next house, okay?"

The friends quickened their pace, dashing from one house to the next and trying to ignore the strange noises and shadows that seemed to be following them. Timmy couldn't help but glance over his shoulder every few seconds, half-expecting to see a monster or a ghost lurking in the darkness.

Finally, they reached the last house on the block. Timmy rang the doorbell, trying to catch his breath.

The door swung open, and a kind-looking old lady stood on the porch, holding a big bowl of candy. "Well, hello there, little ones! Happy Halloween!"

Timmy mustered up his bravest superhero smile. "Trick-or-treat!" he said, holding out his bag.

The old lady smiled and began dropping handfuls of candy into the bags and buckets of the three friends. "My, my, what wonderful costumes! You all look so festive."

As Timmy took a step back, he suddenly felt something brush against his leg. He gasped and looked down, half-expecting to see a monster or a ghost.

But it was just the same little orange cat from the creepy house! The cat meowed and rubbed up against Timmy's ankle, purring softly.

Timmy let out a relieved laugh. "Hey there, little guy. I guess you followed us, huh?"

The old lady chuckled. "Oh, that's just my cat, Pumpkin. He likes to roam the neighborhood on Halloween. I hope he didn't scare you!"

Timmy shook his head and reached down to give the cat a gentle pat. "No, he's not scary at all. He's actually kind of cute."

With one final meow, Pumpkin scampered back into the shadows, disappearing into the night. Timmy, Sarah, and Jared waved goodbye to the old lady and continued on their way, their bags and buckets now overflowing with delicious Halloween candy.

As they walked, Timmy couldn't help but feel a little silly about getting so spooked earlier. It was just the wind and the flickering lights, nothing more. And that silly orange cat had turned out to be the least scary thing all night.

Timmy grinned and hugged his superhero cape a little tighter. "Happy Halloween, you guys!" he said, and the three friends burst out laughing, ready to enjoy the rest of their spooktacular adventure.

Winifred Spooky Halloween

Once upon a time, in a spooky town filled with cobweb-covered houses and mischievous spirits, there lived a witch named Winifred. Now, Winifred was quite a peculiar witch. Instead of using her magic for wicked deeds, she had a mischievous streak and loved to play harmless pranks on the townspeople.

Winifred would brew up a special potion every Halloween that made everyone's costumes come to life. It was a hilarious sight to see as vampires danced, ghosts giggled, and pumpkins hopped around town. The townspeople had come to expect and enjoy Winifred's mischievous tricks, and they eagerly awaited the Halloween festivities each year.

However, there was a grumpy old man named Mr. Snoots who lived in the town. He despised Halloween and believed that it was a violation of his personal beliefs. He thought it was his duty to put an end to all the Halloween fun. So, he decided to confront Winifred and demand that she stop her magical antics.

Mr. Snoots marched up to Winifred's cottage, waving a pamphlet about the First Amendment in his hand. "This Halloween nonsense must stop!" he exclaimed. "It goes against my beliefs, and I demand that you cease your magical activities immediately!"

Winifred, being a mischievous witch with a sense of humor, couldn't help but find Mr. Snoots' seriousness amusing. She let out a cackle and replied, "Oh, Mr. Snoots, you're taking this Halloween business far too seriously! It's all in good fun.

Mr. Snoots huffed and puffed, clearly not amused. It's an infringement on my rights to have these shenanigans happening in my town!"

With a twinkle in her eye, Winifred decided to teach Mr. Snoots a lesson about the lighthearted nature of Halloween. She waved her wand, and in a puff of smoke, Mr. Snoots found himself dressed as a giant pumpkin, complete with a goofy grin and a stem on his head.

"Now, Mr. Snoots, let's see if you can still grumble when you're the life of the Halloween party!" Winifred exclaimed, laughing heartily.

Mr. Snoots, now transformed and surrounded by chuckling townspeople, realized the absurdity of his seriousness. He couldn't help but laugh at his pumpkin-like appearance and the joyous atmosphere around him.

Then, he understood the true spirit of Halloween – a time for fun, laughter, and embracing the freedom of expression.

As the night went on, Mr. Snoots joined in the festivities, dancing with the animated costumes and even bobbing for apples with glee. He discovered that the First Amendment protected not only his right to express his beliefs but also the rights of others to celebrate and have fun.

From that day forward, Mr. Snoots became a more lighthearted and accepting member of the community. He even embraced dressing up for Halloween, becoming known for his creative and often hilarious costumes.

The Best Halloween Ever

It was the night before Halloween, and little Sammy couldn't wait for the big day. He had spent weeks planning the perfect costume - a fuzzy panda bear! Sammy loved pandas and could hardly contain his excitement about going trick-or-treating as one.

Earlier that day, Sammy had helped his mom carve a big jack-o-lantern for the front porch. They had carefully scooped out the seeds and used a knife to carve a silly, toothy grin on the pumpkin's face. Sammy thought it looked absolutely perfect.

As the sun started to set, Sammy put on his panda costume and began jumping around the house, pretending to munch on bamboo leaves. "Look at me, I'm a big, cuddly panda bear!" he giggled.

Sammy's mom laughed. "You sure do look adorable, sweetie! Are you ready to go trick-or-treating with your friends?"

Sammy nodded enthusiastically. "Yes, I can't wait! I'm going to get so much candy!"

Soon, the doorbell rang as the neighborhood kids arrived, all dressed in their spookiest and silliest costumes. Sammy's best friends, Lily the ladybug and Tommy the superhero, were there to greet him.

"Wow, Sammy, your costume is so cute!" Lily exclaimed, admiring the fluffy black-and-white fur.

"Thanks! You look awesome too," Sammy replied. Before heading into the crisp autumn night, the three friends posed for a quick picture.

As they walked from house to house, Sammy couldn't believe how much candy he was collecting. Each neighbor seemed delighted by his panda costume, and they happily dropped handfuls of chocolate, gummy bears, and lollipops into his bag.

"This is the best Halloween ever!" Sammy shouted as they turned the corner.

Suddenly, a loud meow made the kids jump in surprise. A little black cat with green eyes was sitting on the porch of the next house, watching the trick-or-treaters curiously.

"Aww, hello there!" Lily cooed, reaching out to pet the cat. "Aren't you just the cutest thing?"

The cat meowed again and rubbed against Lily's leg, purring softly. Sammy giggled and gave the cat a gentle pat on the head.

"I think he likes us!" Tommy said with a smile.

Just then, the front door of the house opened, and an elderly woman stepped out, holding a big bowl of candy. "Well, look at all you wonderful trick-or-treaters!" she exclaimed. "And who's this friendly little feline keeping you company?"

"He just showed up and started following us," Lily explained. "He's so sweet!"

The old woman chuckled. "That's my cat, Midnight. He loves Halloween and always comes out to greet the neighborhood kids." She held out the bowl of candy.

"Here you go, my dears. Happy Halloween!"

The three friends happily took handfuls of candy, thanking the kind woman. As they continued down the street, Midnight trotted along beside them, occasionally meowing or darting ahead to investigate the next house.

Sammy couldn't believe his luck. Not only was he having the best Halloween ever, but he also had a new furry friend to share it with. He giggled and gave Midnight a gentle pat, his panda ears bouncing with every step.

When the trick-or-treating was finally over, and the kids returned home, Sammy's mom was amazed by how much candy he had collected. "Wow, sweetie, you must have been the hit of the neighborhood in that adorable panda costume!"

Sammy nodded, grinning from ear to ear. "It was the best Halloween ever, Mom! And I even made a new friend - a black cat named Midnight."

As he dumped out his bag of candy and began sorting through the different treats,

Sammy couldn't help but feel incredibly grateful.

He had the best costume, the best friends, and the best Halloween night anyone could ask for. With a contented sigh, he popped a gummy bear into his mouth and settled in to enjoy the rest of the spooky, sweet celebration.

Through the Mist

Deep in the heart of a dense, eerie forest, a thick mist shrouded the landscape. Within that mist, a wicked witch named Malvoria resided in a dilapidated cottage. With a twisted grin and burning eyes, she reveled in darkness and chaos.

The mist thickened on a moonlit Halloween night, and the townspeople felt a chill in their bones. They had heard whispers of Malvoria's wickedness, but fear held them captive, preventing anyone from confronting her directly.

Malvoria's black cat, a creature with piercing yellow eyes and a sinister aura, was her loyal companion. The cat was said to possess mysterious powers, amplifying the witch's malevolence.

Driven by an insatiable desire to spread misery, Malvoria concocted a potent brew of lies and deceit. She whispered her twisted rumors into the wind, which carried them through the town, infecting the hearts and minds of the unsuspecting residents.

As the rumors spread, the once vibrant and kind-hearted community became divided. Neighbors turned against one another, friendships crumbled, and suspicion ran rampant. The atmosphere of the town grew heavy with fear and mistrust.

But amidst the chaos, a young girl named Emily stood tall. She refused to succumb to the darkness that Malvoria had unleashed. With her heart full of courage, Emily embarked on a perilous journey to confront the witch and put an end to her wickedness.

Through the dense mist, she ventured, guided by an inner light that refused to be extinguished. Emily's determination led her to the witch's cottage, where she found Malvoria brewing her toxic lies in a cauldron, her black cat by her side.

With unwavering resolve, Emily confronted the witch, her voice steady and strong. She spoke of the pain and suffering caused by Malvoria's actions, pleading for kindness and unity to restore the town to its former glory.

Malvoria scoffed, her cackling laughter echoing through the cottage. She conjured dark magic, attempting to turn Emily into a Halloween frog as a warning to others who dared challenge her.

But Emily, drawing upon her inner strength, held out a pendant passed down through generations. Bathed in a warm, radiant light, the pendant shielded her from Malvoria's spell. The witch's dark magic rebounded, enveloping her and her malevolent cat in a swirling vortex of shadows.

As the vortex dissipated, the mist began to clear, and the town slowly emerged from its haze of fear. Inspired by Emily's bravery, the people came together, dispelling Malvoria's lies with acts of kindness and understanding.

From that day forward, the town thrived, its unity and compassion serving as a beacon of light that banished the darkness that had consumed them. Malvoria and her black cat were never seen again, a cautionary tale of the consequences of spreading hatred and deceit.

And so, the town lived on, forever changed by the courageous actions of one young girl. The witch's cottage remained a symbol of triumph over darkness, a reminder that kindness and unity will always prevail in the face of wickedness.

Remember, this story is meant to send shivers down your spine on Halloween night. But let it serve as a reminder to choose kindness over cruelty and love over fear.

THE PROTECTOR OF MOORE

PROLOGUE

At 3 AM, Mr. Clark heard his 10-year-old son Tommy scream. He and Mrs. Clark rushed to Tommy's room, but the door wouldn't budge.

"Tommy? We're here!" Mr. Clark called.

"What's wrong?" Mrs. Clark asked anxiously.

"It won't open," he replied.

"Do something, James!" Mrs. Clark cried. Mr. Clark ran at the door, but it suddenly swung open, and he fell hard on the floor. Mrs. Clark rushed to Tommy, who lay silently staring at the ceiling.

"Tommy, are you okay?" she asked.

"Oh, I'm fine!" Mr. Clark said, getting up painfully.

"Mom? Dad? What are you doing here?" Tommy asked, as if nothing had happened.

"James, I'm done! WE NEED TO LEAVE LIKE THE DOCTORS SAID," Mrs. Clark said.

"Leave where, Mom?" Tommy asked, still not moving.

Mr. Clark sat on the bed and explained he had found a new place.

"That's fantastic. We'll leave tomorrow!" Mrs. Clark said with mixed emotions.

The summer had been hard. Tommy was once a normal kid, but since the start of summer break, he'd been having nightmares almost every night. His face grew paler by the day.

After many doctor visits, one suggested they move to a quieter town. They didn't take the advice seriously at first, but Tommy's condition worsened daily. Eventually, they decided it was time.

"Dad? Where are we going?" Tommy asked.

"I found a place with lots of trees, open spaces, and kids your age. It's a little town called M—"

"MOORE?" Tommy interrupted.

"How did you know that?" Mr. Clark was astonished.

Tommy explained he heard it in a dream. It was one of his better dreams, joking that someone misspelled "MORE" and decided, "Yeah! MOORE sounds like a nice name for a town!"

The next day, they packed everything into their truck and checked the house one last time. Mrs. Clark decided to give a one final look, just to ensure everything was packed, and noticed something in Tommy's room.

"James, you might want to see this," Mrs. Clark said, pointing to the roof.

Mr. Clark looked up and felt chills. Scrawled on the ceiling were the words, "SEE YOU IN MOORE!"

THE TOWN OF MOORE

It was October 28th, just three days away from Halloween. Tommy woke up after a long drive and saw they had pulled up in front of a cozy house. He glanced around and noticed a dense forest in the distance. Before he could take in the scenery, nature called.

"Mom! Bathroom!" he yelled, jumping out of the truck.

"Straight in, second door to your right," Mrs. Clark pointed, busy unloading. Tommy rushed inside and grabbed the bathroom door handle, twisting it urgently.

"OCCUPADO!" came his dad's voice.

"DAD! I REALLY NEED TO GO!"

"Yeah, I didn't come here for make-up either, son. You gotta wait your turn," Mr. Clark joked.

After what felt like an eternity, the door opened, and Tommy dashed in, slamming it behind him.

"Whoa! Somebody really needed to go, huh?" Mr. Clark chuckled.

"OCCUPADO!" Tommy shouted from inside. Mr. Clark laughed, feeling relieved to see Tommy acting normally.

Outside, the friendly neighbors, the Smiths, were helping the new family move in. The Smiths were in their 50s but looked younger and had a son, Jake, a year older than Tommy.

After what felt like an eternity, Tommy finally came out of the bathroom and thought to help his parents move their stuff inside.

"Tommy, say hello to our new neighbors, the Smiths, and their son, Jake!" Mrs. Clark called.

"Hello!" Tommy waved, descending the front steps.

Tommy tried to talk to Jake, but Jake was quiet. Instead, they listened to their parents discuss the town's highlights.

"What about the forest? Does it have a lake?" Tommy asked.

The smiles vanished. It was as if he'd said something taboo.

"Oh, we'll explore the woods later, son," Mr. Clark said.

"But I want—" Tommy began, but Mr. Smith put a hand on his shoulder, smiling.

"You best avoid the woods, especially this time of year," Mr. Smith advised.

Sensing tension, Mrs. Clark changed the subject. "Why don't we all step inside for a nice cup of coffee?"

"We have coffee?" Mr. Clark asked excitedly.

"We Have Coffee!" Mrs. Clark replied, puzzled. "You did pack the coffee maker and beans, right?"

"Jake, this is when my dad gets in trouble. Mom says he has the memory of a goldfish!" Tommy whispered, giggling.

"I thought you said to get coffee once we got here," Mr. Clark protested.

"No, darling. I said Make Sure to Get the Coffee, period!" Mrs. Clark corrected.

"Oh, that's not good!" Jake giggled louder.

"Don't worry! As our new neighbors, why don't you come over? We've got coffee, wine, and a barbeque going on too!" Mrs. Smith offered.

After moving the final box, the Clarks went to the Smiths' home and had a great time. Later that night, around 11 PM, they returned home, finally ready for a well-deserved sleep after a full day and full bellies.

THE COSTUME DISASTERS

"Day after tomorrow's Halloween! Just two days remaining." Tommy thought, eager to see the town's Halloween spirit and creativity. He loved the thrill of being scared.

As he looked out his large window, the night was dark, with warm tones from street lights and lanterns. Beyond that, it was pitch black.

Tommy struggled to sleep in the new place, feeling uneasy about the unfamiliar surroundings. The dark forest with its tall trees didn't exactly help either. He turned away from the jagged line of tall, motionless trees.

"Dumb trees, probably thinking, 'Oooo, look at me, how tall I am.'" He tried to laugh to relax. Soon, he fell asleep and had a good night's sleep for the first time in weeks.

The next morning, he woke up feeling energetic and fresh. After his morning routine, he greeted his parents with a big hug and sat down for breakfast.

"Someone's in a great mood?" Mrs. Clark said, messing up Tommy's hair.

"Yeah! I finally found the coffee beans," Mr. Clark said. Both Tommy and his mother looked at him somewhat puzzled. "Oh, you meant Tommy, not… Never mind!" Mr. Clark, somewhat embarrassed, looked away.

"I'm fine, Mom! I feel like moving here really worked."

"I sure hope so!" Mrs. Clark said.

"Son, you're 10, right?" Mr. Clark asked.

"Duh!" Tommy responded, making a funny face.

"Great! You're a man now, and a man needs coffee in the morning. Let's get you some!"

Mrs. Clark wasn't sure this was a good idea but decided to watch. Mr. Clark poured coffee into a small cup and placed it on the table.

"Go on, son! Have at it!"

Tommy, excited to be a man, took a big sip and regretted it immediately.

"*pphhhhrrrtttt* WHAT IS THIS STUFF?"

"That, son, is a man's drink!"

"Dad! It tastes more like something a horse would have. It's disgusting." Tommy complained, cleaning his tongue with a paper towel.

With breakfast done, Tommy told his parents he'd explore the town on his skateboard and hopefully make new friends. The small town meant he wouldn't get lost.

Tommy set out and instantly noticed the festive decorations: lights, Jack-O-Lanterns, and spider webs on poles.

"I'm really looking forward to seeing great costumes," Tommy thought as he set off.

Soon, he came across some kids preparing their costumes in the park. The whole town seemed to be helping each other out.

"ROAARRRRRRR!!!!!" A kid jumped out of the bushes.

"Whoa!" Somewhat startled. "You're a gingerbread man! Nice work!" Tommy said, startled.

"Ginger what? No! I'm a bear!" the kid explained, annoyed.

"Righttttt! Well, have fun!" Tommy said, disappointed, and continued forward.

He came across another kid sitting on a low wall. He waved, and she waved back.

"You're the new kid in town, aren't you?" she asked.

"Yeah! And you're the new snowman of Moore?" Tommy couldn't help himself.

"Snowman? I'm Humpty Dumpty!" she exclaimed.

"Yeah, I meant that…" Tommy was again disappointed by another failed costume attempt.

All day, Tommy saw kids in uninspired costumes. Heading home, he missed his old city.

"At least they knew the difference between a gingerbread man and a bear." Suddenly, a chill ran through his body. The wind grew colder, and dark clouds covered the sky, even though it was just 4 PM.

"That's odd!" Tommy thought as he skateboarded home.

He heard a clickity-clack sound and stopped, feeling a strange urge to look around.

CLICKITY-CLACK

"A horse?" Tommy turned to see.

It was a black, majestic stallion stepping out of a fog, tall and strong. Tommy's heart sank in fear. The horse had red glowing eyes, and a headless figure in old-fashioned hunter's clothes rode it, a sharp sword hanging at its side.

"Okay! Sir, Mam! You got me! That's really impressive!" Tommy remembered it was Halloween and thought someone was practicing their costume, but he couldn't shake the fright. The dark clouds and fog added to the eerie atmosphere.

"Why isn't he moving?" Tommy thought, growing more terrified. He decided to rush back home.

"Okay. I'm gonna head back home now." Tommy turned to run but found the figure just an arm's reach away. A headless man and his horse loomed over him. Before he could react, everything went black.

THE OLD MAN

Tommy woke up feeling ravenous, realizing he'd been out cold for an entire day. He was surrounded by people, some familiar, some not.

"Mom! I'm hungry," Tommy said softly.

"We found you on the side of the road and spent the whole day trying to wake you up," his mom explained, hugging him tightly. "I'll get your breakfast!"

"I passed out for a day?" Tommy asked.

"Yes, son. We think you slipped and hit your head or something," Mr. Clark said, setting up a tray with Tommy's breakfast.

"And who are these people?" Tommy looked around.

"They came to see you, honey," his mom said lovingly.

Everyone speculated how Tommy had fainted or injured himself, but Tommy kept thinking, "That's not what happened."

"What happened, son?" his mom asked, more concerned.

"I… I think I saw a ghost!" Tommy said, making the room grow silent.

"Son, you probably saw someone in a costume. Everyone's been busy practicing their Halloween costumes," Mr. Clark said.

"No! DAD! I saw a ghost. A headless man and…"

"A what now? Headless?" said Mr. Smith, the neighbor.

Everyone laughed, suggesting Tommy had mistaken one of the street pole witch effigies. Furious, Tommy noticed an old man in the corner, smiling and gesturing for him to stay quiet.

"Is he picking his nose or telling me to stay quiet?" Tommy thought.

"Here, let me take this away. Why don't you get some fresh air?" Mom stepped between him and the old man, blocking Tommy's view.

Later, in the park, Tommy observed everyone's costume preparations. As he approached the entrance, he saw a familiar figure on a bench.

"It's you!" Tommy exclaimed. It was the old man from earlier.

"Why did you tell me to keep quiet?" Tommy asked.

"Well, we don't want to alarm the town. What you saw was real," the man said in a high-pitched but soft tone.

"You mean there really is a headless horseman?" Tommy inquired.

"Yes! He was once the protector of Moore, killed by a demon wanting to take over the town."

"A demon?" Tommy felt more excited than scared.

"The headless horseman was the only thing standing between the demon and the town."

"What happened to him?" Tommy asked curiously.

"They hired someone to kill him. All they found was the body. His head was never found."

"I felt like he wanted to speak to me."

"If he had a head, he probably would!" laughed the old man.

"You need to warn the children. The elders won't believe you, but the children will. Keep them home on Halloween!" the old man warned.

A thunderclap rang in the distance, startling Tommy. When he turned back, the old man had vanished. Tommy saw a note where the man had been. It read: Help Them!

The wind grew strong, an eerie fog settled in, and the skies turned red.

"Okay, this is creepy!" Tommy told himself, hopping on his bike. But figures emerged from the fog. Numerous, pale, ghostly, with unsettling grins and pointy teeth.

Tommy decided to ditch his bike and run. He fell hard, paralyzed with fear. The rain came down hard, muffling his screams. He looked up to see the figures approaching. Then, he felt someone breathing next to his ear, whispering: "Tomorrow – We Shall Return!"

"GO AWAY!!!!" Tommy screamed.

Rapid thuds approached. He turned to see the headless horseman and his horse.

"Are you here to kill me?" Tommy asked, faint with fear.

The horseman signaled no.

"Are you protecting me?" The horse reared, and the horseman bowed slightly. With one move, the horseman charged at the ghostly figures, who retreated into the fog.

Tommy stood and picked up his bike, ready to leave. But his parents stood in front of him, eyes wide with fear.

"Who was that, Tommy?" Mom asked.

"Tell me that wasn't just some stranger trying to hurt you," Dad said.

"No! He helped me. He's protecting me. I told you but you wouldn't listen," Tommy tried to explain.

"We have to call the cops," his mother insisted.

"Let's not rush into things. It was probably just someone pranking Tommy. Let's go home. It's windy and wet outside," Dad said, trying to calm everyone.

HALLOWEEN EVE

The Clarks were visibly shaken, unable to make sense of what they saw the other day. They were especially concerned for Tommy's safety now that it was Halloween.

"We should've called the cops. If someone thinks they can scare Tommy like that, they're mistaken," Mrs. Clark insisted.

"Oh, come on! You're overreacting a little. Relax. No one would want to hurt our boy," said Mr. Clark.

"Yeah, I guess you're right," Mrs. Clark sighed.

"Now, how about we get ready for the kids? I've got a surprise for them this year," Mr. Clark said with a grin.

"Let me guess, the faceless man again?" Mrs. Clark asked sarcastically.

"Oh, come on! It's faceless, not headless. I get to stand still, kids get scared, and I can nap without anyone noticing," Mr. Clark explained, clearly excited.

"Whatever, darling! As long as you don't walk into the neighbor's pool like last time, I'm okay with it."

"Hey! That's not fair. I couldn't see and it was dark," defended Mr. Clark.

Tommy came downstairs, feeling different.

"Sweetie! Are you okay?" his mother asked with genuine concern.

"Oh, yes, Mom. I'm okay," Tommy said with a smile. He felt assured he had no reason to be afraid anymore.

"What's so funny?" asked his dad, walking out of the kitchen in a white faceless mask.

"Uh, Dad! That's a painting," Tommy said, holding back laughter as he saw his dad facing a painting of a child sitting in a chair.

"I totally knew that," said Mr. Clark, immediately turning around and still facing the wrong direction.

As the family had their breakfast, they couldn't help but notice noises from their neighbors. At first, they thought it was just the kids having fun, but soon, the screams grew louder. Police sirens started approaching their street.

"What's going on?" Tommy inquired, getting up to check.

Mr. Clark opened the door and signaled his family to stay inside, but Mrs. Clark and Tommy stepped outside before him.

"Wait for me!" Mr. Clark said, trying to quickly take off his mask.

It looked like the entire town had gathered in the park across their house. Tommy could hear people crying, yelling, and screaming. Something terrible had happened, and Tommy immediately connected the dots.

"Tomorrow – We Shall Return."

Tommy knew this had to be related to the ghosts or demons he saw the other day before the Horseman came to help.

As they reached the crowd, Mr. Clark started asking everyone what was going on, but people were too busy hugging each other, crying, and calling out to their children.

"Where are all the kids?" Mrs. Clark asked, sensing the obvious. She grabbed Tommy's hand tightly.

"YOU! YOU SHOULD HAVE NEVER COME HERE!" someone from the crowd pointed at the Clarks.

"I'm sorry, what?" Mr. Clark, clearly confused, asked.

"Your child – WHY? WHATEVER DID WE DO TO YOU?" This person was crying profusely, and Tommy couldn't understand why he was being singled out.

As they made their way to the center, many townsfolk blamed them for the catastrophe.

"Don't you get it! THEY TOOK OUR CHILDREN, ALL OF THEM!" said Mrs. Smith, shaking Tommy. Tommy was frightened.

"LEAVE HIM ALONE. HE HAS DONE NOTHING," Mrs. Clark defended Tommy while making their way through.

At the center of the crowd was a raised platform, almost like an altar but with no statue or symbols. On it stood a few police officers and the mayor of the town.

"Alright! Calm down, everyone! We're working on it and we'll find your children, all of them," the mayor explained on a megaphone, but it did little to calm the crowd.

"No, you won't!" said Tommy, and everyone started looking at him.

"Tommy, be quiet," Mr. Clark covered his mouth, hoping to prevent more trouble.

"No, DAD! EVERYONE NEEDS TO LISTEN TO ME. I THINK I KNOW WHAT'S GOING ON!"

"What do you mean, son?" the mayor asked.

"The demons from the forest. I know they're behind all of this."

"Not this again, Tommy. There are no demons, okay?" Tommy's mother was getting agitated.

"No, you don't understand. The Horseman, he's trying to help us. MOM, DAD! YOU NEED TO BELIEVE ME!"

The parents chose to ignore what Tommy said, thinking it was just a child's imagination.

Tommy was angry, but he knew he had to act. If he didn't, something terrible would happen to the missing children, the town, and his parents.

"I'm not gonna let that happen." Tommy pulled his hand back and ran toward the forest.

"Tommy, TOMMY! YOU GET BACK HERE RIGHT NOW!" Mrs. Clark started yelling and running after him.

The mayor focused on handling the crowd, but Mr. and Mrs. Clark ran after Tommy, clearly not good runners.

Tommy ran as fast as he could. He could hear his parents' yells growing more distant as he neared the forest.

"WHAT AM I DOING? I'M JUST A 10-YEAR-OLD. I DIDN'T SIGN UP FOR THIS!" he thought, but he knew he was the only one who could do something about it.

The trees grew taller and taller as he got closer. He found a passage into the forest and went in without hesitation. His parents' screams grew faint and incomprehensible.

As Tommy ran through the dense bushes and trees, he realized the forest was getting creepier. He stopped to catch his breath, clueless about which direction to take. He was surrounded by thick trees. After a quick look, he found an opening just big enough for him to squeeze through.

"WHERE ARE YOU GUYS?" Tommy screamed, hoping for a response. He started hearing cries of children, many of them.

"I'M COMING!" Tommy followed the voices, which grew louder. Just when he thought he was close, the voices stopped. Realizing this was probably a trap, Tommy stopped and didn't dare move. No sound, not even the wind. No footsteps, no parents yelling his name — nothing!

"Okay, this is not good!" Tommy thought, feeling the fear grow inside him. Then, a faint noise emerged.

"Someone's laughing?" Tommy said. The laughter grew louder and started coming from all directions. The ground felt mushy, like he was standing on wet, slippery mud. He looked down and saw a pale skull staring back at him with empty eye sockets.

A hand emerged from the tree next to Tommy and grabbed his arm. Another hand grabbed his leg and pulled. Tommy fell sideways onto the mud, which now had puddles of water. The laughter grew louder, making him want to cover his ears.

"So, you've finally come!" a dark, demonic voice rang through the area.

THE EVIL WITHIN THE WOODS

Tommy was paralyzed with fear. He mustered enough strength to look around. Just a few yards away, a puddle, deep red like boiling blood, began to bubble furiously.

"After all this time, I get to see you and finish you," the demonic voice said. From the puddle emerged a massive entity with horns, a trident in its left hand, and a skull in its right. Its skin was as red as blood, its teeth looked capable of ripping Tommy apart.

"Oh, boy! I'm done!" Tommy thought.

"Where's your friend now, child?" asked a voice next to Tommy.

"Oh, come to save your friends, have we?" laughed another voice.

"You need to let them go, and I promise I won't hurt you!" Tommy said bravely, making every demon laugh.

"The last time someone tried to hurt me, I cut his head off," the demon leader said, looking at the skull in his hand.

"That's the Headless Horseman's head? So, he wasn't always headless!" Tommy said.

"Your friend won't be stopping us this time!" The demon approached Tommy, swinging his trident.

He stopped next to Tommy. The smaller demons picked Tommy up and forced him to kneel. Still struggling to free himself, Tommy saw the demon raising the trident high above him.

"Now, I take back… WHAT'S MINE!" Tommy closed his eyes, thinking of his parents, and why the horseman didn't save him.

THE HORSEMAN RIDES AGAIN

SHHWWWWIINNGGGGG The sound of an unsheathed sword echoed in the forest, followed by the neigh of a horse.

"WHAT? IMPOSSIBLE!" the demonic figure said, red eyes wide in disbelief as he stared at the Headless Horseman riding towards him with his sword.

The demons scrambled, letting go of Tommy. The demon lord took a few steps back, still trying to comprehend how the Horseman still rode. The Horseman stopped right next to Tommy.

"You should seriously consider delivering pizzas—you'd make a fortune," Tommy said, feeling relieved and empowered as he climbed onto the back of the horse. The Horseman and Tommy now rode together.

The Horseman and the horse knocked out many demons while Tommy looked on in sheer excitement.

"Hey! Where's my sword?" he asked, and just as he said that, the Horseman stopped and gently swung his arm behind to hand over the sword to Tommy. It was then that Tommy realized why the demon wanted him dead.

"So, you want me to kill the demon?" The horse reared, almost making Tommy lose his balance and fall.

"I'll take that as a yes. Mr. Horseman, sir! Let's get him!" Tommy pointed his heavy sword towards the demon king with both hands, and the Horseman responded by turning his horse and heading straight towards the demon.

"PROTECT ME, YOU FOOLS!" screamed the demon as he retreated, but no one dared step up.

As soon as they reached striking distance, it felt like time slowed down, just like in the games Tommy played on his computer. He grabbed the handle tightly, pointed the sword forward, never once blinking to remain focused, and thrust it right through the demon.

"NOOOOOOO!!!! IT CANNOT BE!" screamed the demon with his blood-curdling voice as he started to disintegrate into smoke.

THE PROTECTOR OF MOORE

Tommy looked around, breathing heavily, and saw the eerie mist lifting from the forest. The demons hiding behind trees were disintegrating, revealing regular children, crying and frightened. Tommy handed the sword to the Horseman, jumped down, and ran towards the kids. "Hey, hey! You're okay. They won't harm you now," Tommy reassured the children, helping them up. Many followed Tommy and the Horseman.

"So, it's over?" asked one of the kids.

"Yes! Thanks to him!" Tommy pointed to the Horseman. The kids, though frightened by the headless figure, felt relieved. They were free from the evil that had trapped them.

Tommy heard a familiar voice. "WHERE ARE YOU?" It was his mom.

"MOM!! I'M HERE!" Tommy ran towards the voice. Sure enough, it was his mother and father, on their knees, out of breath. He hugged them tightly.

"We were so worried, son. We thought we lost you," his mom said, tears rolling down her cheeks.

"You don't have to worry anymore, Mom. I had help!" Tommy pointed to the Horseman approaching them. At first, his parents were frightened, but then they saw hundreds of children following him out of the woods.

"You…!" Mr. Clark said before breaking down in tears.

"Thank you," said Mr. Clark. The Horseman bowed to acknowledge the respect.

The Horseman led everyone out of the woods and into the town. The entire town stood in front of the forest entrance, in disbelief at what they were witnessing. Parents rushed in to grab and hug their children, relieved to see them safe. The Horseman stood with Tommy, watching the reunions.

Tommy's mom squeezed his hand, silently saying, "You did it, son!"

The mayor and the police approached Tommy and the Horseman cautiously.

"Told you!" said Tommy with a proud grin. The mayor smiled, still unsure if the Headless Horseman was an ally or a foe. "They saved our children. They're the protectors of Moore," someone in the crowd said, starting to clap. Soon, everyone was applauding Tommy and the Horseman.

"Well, it looks like you won't be needing us anymore, Miss Mayor," said a police officer.

"That, I won't. We've got a protector of our own!" said the mayor with pride. The Horseman bowed to show his appreciation. Tommy got off the horse and started clapping for the new hero. The Horseman turned towards him, raised a finger to where his lips would have been, asking Tommy to be quiet.

"YOU! You're the old man?" Tommy realized the truth.

The Horseman turned, raised his sword high, and rode into the distance until he was no longer visible.

Since that day, Tommy never had nightmares. He became friends with every kid in town. Everyone knew him and wanted to be with him. The Horseman would ride every now and then in the evening, ensuring everyone was protected. People waved at him, and some tried to take a picture, only to find it wasn't possible. Nobody was scared—everyone loved their new protector.

To honor the heroes, the mayor raised enough money to build a statue at the entrance of the park near Tommy's home. The statue was tall, depicting Tommy, the Headless Horseman, and the horse riding. At the foot of the statue was a plaque that read:

The Protectors of Moore –
The Headless Horseman and Tommy!

Wishing you a spine-chilling,
heart-pounding, frightfully fun
Halloween
that's full of screams and thrills!